WALT DISNEY
MICKEY MOUSE ADVENTURES

S0-ANG-431

TAKE-ALONG COMIC

GEMSTONE PUBLISHING
TIMONIUM, MARYLAND

STEPHEN A. GEPPI
*President/Publisher and
Chief Executive Officer*

JOHN K. SNYDER JR.
Chief Administrative Officer

STAFF

LEONARD (JOHN) CLARK
Editor-in-Chief

GARY LEACH
Associate Editor

SUE KOLBERG
Assistant Editor

TRAVIS SEITLER
Art Director

SUSAN DAIGLE-LEACH
Production Associate

DAVID GERSTEIN
Archival Editor

MELISSA BOWERSOX
Director-Creative Projects

• IN THIS ISSUE •

Mickey Mouse
Project Volcania
Story & Art: Guiseppe Zironi
Translation and dialogue: Dwight Decker
Lettering: Sue Kolberg

Donald Duck
Crystal Ball
Story: Spectrum Associates **Art:** Bancells

Mickey Mouse
Colder Than Ice
Story: Michael T. Gilbert
Art: Joaquin

Original interior color by **Egmont**
Lettering by **Jamison Services**
Additional production by **Gary Leach**

**ADVERTISING/
MARKETING**

J.C.VAUGHN
Executive Editor

BRENDA BUSICK
Creative Director

JAMIE DAVID
Director of Marketing

SARA ORTT
Marketing Assistant

HEATHER WINTER
Office Manager
Toll Free
(888) 375-9800 Ext. 249
ads@gemstonepub.com

MARK HUESMAN
Production Assistant

MIKE WILBUR
Shipping Manager

RALPH TURNER
Accounting Manager

**WALT DISNEY'S
MICKEY MOUSE
ADVENTURES 8**
Take-Along Comic
February, 2006

Published by
Gemstone Publishing

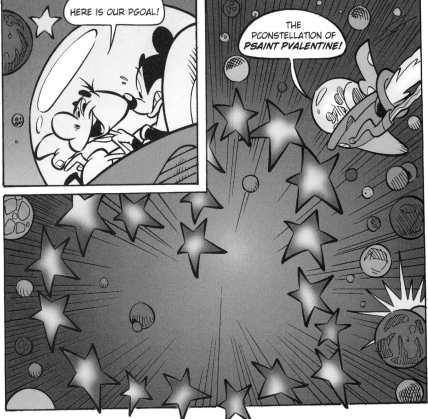

THIS IS OUR PERSONAL *ROBO-PCLERK!*

WELCOME! I AM CUPID-3, AT YOUR SERVICE!

PLEASE ACCOMPANY ME TO THE *SWEETHEART-O-MATIC!*

PSURE!

BLONDE, BRUNETTE... HEIGHT, WEIGHT... NUMBER OF LEGS, NUMBER OF ARMS... PLEASE SELECT!

IT'S HIS *FIRST PTIME!*

SELECT?

HMM... IT DOESN'T SEEM VERY HARD! HEIGHT, COMPLEXION...

PGO ON!

EYES... *TWO*, RIGHT?

PBRAVO!

THE SULFUROUS ATMOSPHERE IN THESE TUNNELS IS THE MOST *FRAGRANT* ON YOUR WHOLE PLANET!

COUGH!

NOW, EARTHLING, IT IS TIME TO MEET HER MOST *SULFUROUS HIGHNESS...*

HIGHNESS...?

...PRINCESS *SULPHURIA!*

MINNIE'S HELMET!

EARTHLING, YOURS IS AN EXCELLENT PRESENT!

FROM THIS DAY FORTH, OUR TWO PEOPLES WILL SURELY ENJOY AN ENDURING FRIENDSHIP!

UH... OF COURSE!

IT IS A VOLCANIAN TRADITION TO RESPECT THE CUSTOMS OF THE HOST PEOPLE!

THEY *SEEM* WELL-INTENTIONED!

EARTH AND VOLCANIA WILL BECOME TWIN PLANETS! THAT IS *PROJECT VOLCANIA!*

YOUR PROBLEMS HAVE BEEN SOLVED IN ONE BLOW!

It Will Give

YOU
X-RAY
VISION

JEEPERS, CREEPERS, WHERE'D YOU GET THOSE PEEPERS?
Yes, one of the most coveted superpowers is now just a click away. Scoop opens your
eyes to the latest ground-breaking news and lets you see beyond the surface of any news
story - learn what the hottest new Batman statue is made of or find out the true origin of
Wolverine. Crammed with powerful character images and the latest industry news,
Scoop is the free weekly e-newsletter from Gemstone Publishing and Diamond
International Galleries that will give you the vision to toast your competition with your
keen insider knowledge and product savvy. So, read Scoop and see your collection soar
to the heights of Superman when you transform your collecting vision from 20/20 to
20/MONEY. Whether you're a pop culture enthusiast or a collecting fiend, visit
http://scoop.diamondgalleries.com to check it all out and subscribe. No bones about it -
Scoop is *ULTRAVIOLETLY FUN!!!*

Crystal Ball

AN UNSYMPATHETIC RESPONSE LATER...

BOY! WAS HE TOUCHY!

SLAM!

HURRAH! IT'S THE RESULTS OF MY CHOCOLATE PUDDING EXAM! I'VE PASSED! WAIT TILL I TELL...

HEY! GUESS WHAT YOUR VERY TALENTED, NOT TO SAY GIFTED, UNCLE DONALD JUST DID?

PASSED HIS CHOCOLATE PUDDING EXAM! A-A-A-A-A...

QUIET, UNCA DONALD! THIS IS A CRITICAL MOMENT!

WE'RE NEARLY FINISHED!

...A-A-A-A-A-ATCHOOOOOOOOO!

...A-A-A-A-A-ATCHO-O-O-O-O!

SO THE SPY'S *HIDING* IN THE VENTILATION SYSTEM, EH? THAT'LL MAKE IT REALLY *EASY*...

...AS ALL I HAFTA DO IS POST A GUARD BY EVERY DUCT! *HA-HA-HA!*

GASP! I GOTTA SKEDADDLE!

AND AT THE FIRST AVAILABLE DUCT...

WHAT LUCK! THERE'S NO ONE POSTED IN HERE!

IT'S DARK IN HERE! *AHA!* HERE'S A LIGHT SWITCH!

THE ONLY UNGUARDED DUCT IS IN THERE, AND *THIS* DOOR'S LOCKED!

X-RAY LAB! KEEP OUT!

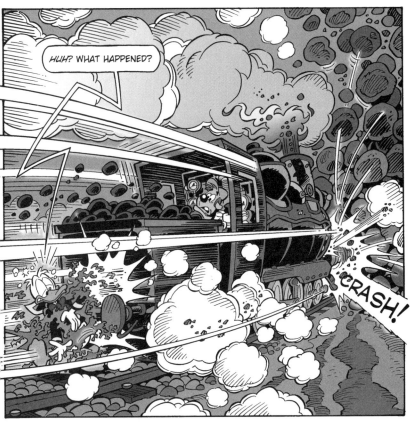

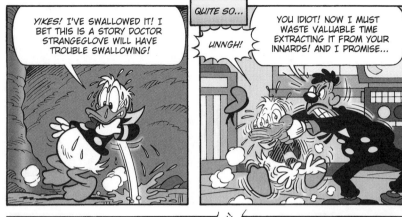

DON'T GAWK! GET HIM!

TIME TO MAKE TRACKS!

GOTTA FIND SOMEONE WHO CAN REIN IN THAT LUNATIC...

THIS IS DOC STRANGEGLOVE! THE INTRUDER IS ON THE LOOSE! FIND HIM AND BRING HIM TO ME!

GULP! I'VE GOT TO SKEDDADLE!

EASIER SAID THAN DONE...

THIS PLACE IS A RABBIT WARREN! LESSEE...

WOW! TAKE A GANDER AT THAT...

THIS WAY, MINISTER! I HAVE SOMETHING TO SHOW YOU!

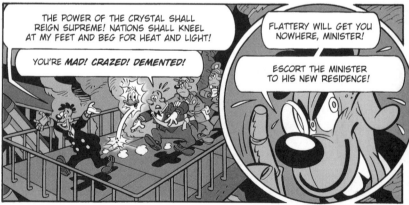

SEEMS THE MINISTER AND I ARE IN THE SAME BOAT! MAYBE WE CAN HELP EACH OTHER!

MOMENTS LATER...

THAT'S TAKES CARE OF HIM! YOU TAKE THE FIRST SHIFT!

SURE THING! IT BEATS DIGGING ROCKS! *YAWN!*

HMM! THIS IS MY CHANCE!

HI! MY NAME'S DONALD!

GASP!

I-I-I MUST BE SEEING THINGS! YOU CAN'T BE REAL!

BUT I AM! HONEST! I JUST HAD THIS ACCIDENT WITH AN X-RAY MACHINE...

A WACKY EXPLANATION LATER...

THANKS TO YOU WE CAN STILL BEAT THAT LUNATIC! I HAVE A PLAN!

YOU DO?

YES! WE HAVE TO ESCAPE THE ISLAND - WITH THE CRYSTAL!

GOOD IDEA! BUT...*UH*...HOW?

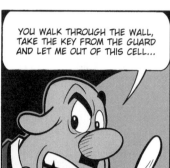

YOU WALK THROUGH THE WALL, TAKE THE KEY FROM THE GUARD AND LET ME OUT OF THIS CELL...

A QUICK KEY SNATCH LATER...

ZZZZZZZZZZ!

BINGO! NOW WE JUST HAVE TO FIND A...

"...SPEEDBOAT!"

THAT'S THE SPEEDBOAT THAT BROUGHT ME HERE! LET'S GET ABOARD AND OUTTA HERE!

SO FAR, SO GOO...

HEY!

YOU, THERE! *STOP!*

...BAD, I MEAN! WE'VE BEEN SPOTTED!

UH-OH!

BUT WHAT CAN YOU DO TO AVOID *THIS?* EEEYOW!

AAAAGH!

CRASH!

SPLASH!

SPLASH!

THE CRYSTAL, PACKED WITH CONDENSED ENERGY, IS A DEAD WEIGHT PULLING DONALD DOWN INTO THE DEPTHS...

OH, NO! HE'S SINKING LIKE A LEAD BALLOON!

GASP! TOO HEAVY...TO SURFACE! IT'S...THE END!

HEY! WHAT'S GOING ON DOWN THERE?

KEEP CALM, WE'LL THROW YOU A LIFE BUOY!

BUT WHERE'S DONALD? HE MUST HAVE SUNK!

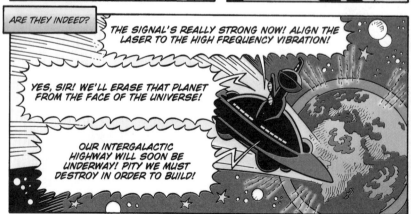

MANY HOURS LATER...

WHAT A DAY! BET THE KIDS ARE REALLY ASHAMED OF ME NOW!

AS WELL AS UNCLE SCROOGE AND...*GULP!*...DAISY! HOPE I CAN SNEAK INTO THE HOUSE UNNOTICED!

I CAN STILL WALK THROUGH WALLS! THAT OUGHTA BE WORTH SOMETHING!

DONK!

UMPH!

GREAT! NOW I CAN'T EVEN DO THAT ANYMORE! CAN THINGS POSSIBLY GET ANY WORSE?

POSSIBLY...

???

SO YOU DON'T THINK I'M USELESS?

NO! WE'RE PROUD OF YOU, UNCA DONALD!

YOU'RE A WINNER!

NOT *ALTOGETHER* USELESS...I SUPPOSE!

AND WE CAN'T WAIT TO HAVE ONE OF YOUR CHOCOLATE PUDDINGS!

THEN I'LL GO AND MAKE THE BEST PUDDING YOU'VE EVER EATEN!

LATER...

MMMMM!

WONDERFUL!

NOT BAD, ALL IN ALL!

A PERFECT END TO A HORRIBLE DAY! SHALL WE GO OUT AND CHECK FOR FALLING STARS, DAISY?

YES, LET'S!

THERE'S ONE NOW! BUT WHAT TO WISH FOR? I MEAN, I'VE GOT EVERYTHING...

HE MOUNTAIN OF YOUTH!

It's all in here!

SpongeBob SquarePants, y Story, Superman, Jimmy Neutron, Spider-Man, oy Rogers, Garfield, Uncle Scrooge, ck Rogers, Pokemon, Small Soldiers, Superhero Resins, atman, Muhammad li, The Lone Ranger, neyana, KISS, Mickey ouse, Puppet Master, Elvis, The Phantom, Men, Charlie Chaplin, e Cisco Kid, Donald ck, Captain Marvel, urel & Hardy, Howdy oody, Planet of the pes, MAD, Hopalong Cassidy, Captain erica, Toy Guns and ore! Many rare and e-of-kind collectibles are included in the ew, expanded and updated listings.

OFFICIAL
Hake's Price Guide to
Character Toys

All characters ©2004 respective copyright holders. All rights reserved.

TO ORDER CALL SARA AT 888-375-9800 EXT. 410

This amazing photo volume contains!

Almost 15,000 items!

Almost 45,000 prices listed!

Every item is pictured!

More than 1,100 pages!

All-new color section!

Expanded and updated listings!

370 unique categories!

Checklist feature!

r centuries, the elusive "fountain of youth" has been just beyond the realm of pos-
bility, but now with the HAKE'S PRICE & PHOTO GUIDE TO CHARACTER TOYS #5, you
n relive your childhood with the help of this all-in-one collectible guide! Stay young
 heart with this mountainous volume packed with nostalgic pricing and pictures!
AKE'S PRICE GUIDE TO CHARACTER TOYS #5 - where youth springs eternal!

ALMOST 15,000 ITEMS SHOWN!

$35 +s&h

I'M OKAY... *BARELY!* THAT *METEOR* ALMOST...

SAY! WHAT'S WITH THE *SNOW?*

YOU TELL ME! THERE'S ICE *EVERYWHERE...*

...EXCEPT WHERE *YOU ARE!*

HUH? FUNNY...I'M NOT *COLD* AT ALL!

BRRRR! I AM! *C-COLD...* AND *SCARED!* SOMETHING'S *W-WRONG...*

THAT METEOR MUST'VE BEEN ONE HUGE *SNOWBALL!* LET'S GO BACK AND WARM UP WITH SOME *HOT COCOA!*

IT'LL TAKE MORE THAN *C-COCOA* T-TO STOP ME *S-SHAKING,* MICKEY!

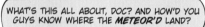

IT MAKES YOU *ABSORB HEAT* THE WAY A *SPONGE* ABSORBS WATER! EVERYTHING NEAR YOU *FREEZES!*

LUCKILY, WE KNEW THE METEOR WOULD BE *SUB-ZERO*, AND WORE THESE *INSULATED SUITS!*

THE *ICE-CREAM* TRUCK WAS *MY* IDEA! *SMART*, HUH?

YEAH! WHO'D NOTICE AN *ICE-CREAM TRUCK* TINKLING AROUND IN THE *FOREST?*

LISTEN, FUNNY-BOY, THE DOC WANTS TO *TEST* YOU! YOU GONNA *COOPERATE* OR NOT?

DO I HAVE ANY *CHOICE?*

NO!

NOW TO SEE HOW *QUICKLY* YOU CAN ABSORB *HEAT!*

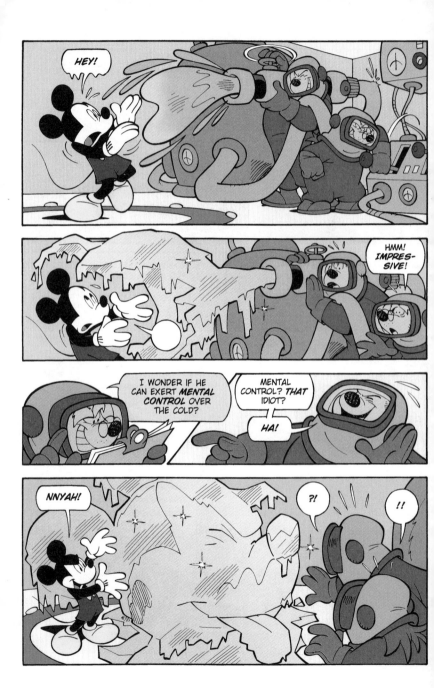

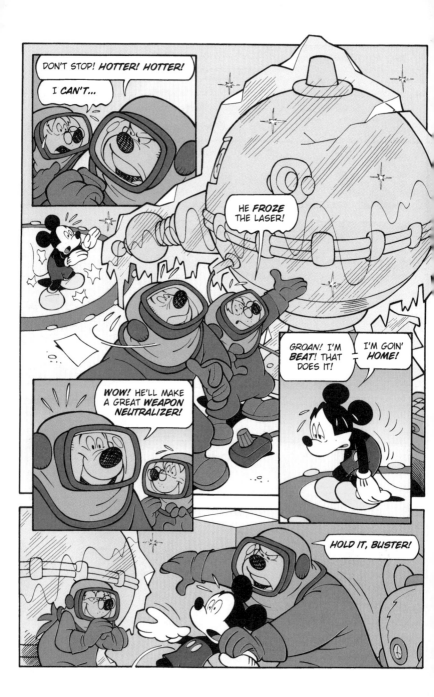

YOU'RE A **SECURITY RISK!** WE **CAN'T** LET YOU GO!

I DID YOUR STUPID **TESTS!** YOU CAN'T KEEP ME HERE!

I SAY I **CAN**...

...AND SO DO **THEY!**

!

NOW KEEP **QUIET** UNTIL WE FIGURE OUT WHAT TO **DO** WITH YOU!

AND SO...

OKAY, FOLLOW ME!

EH? **NOW** WHAT?

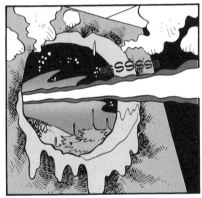

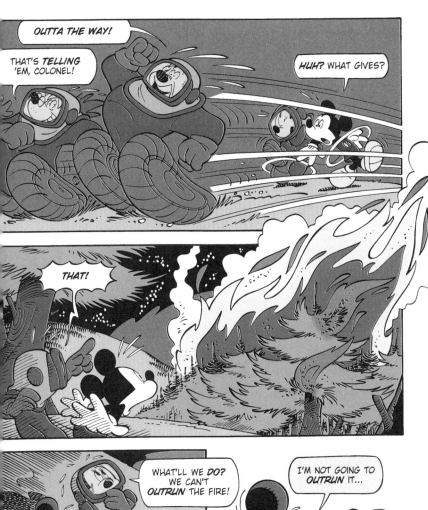

THE INCREDIBLE HULK

WALL STATUE

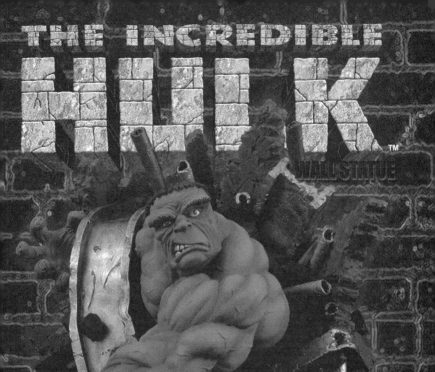

BASED ON *HULK GRAY* **BY JEPH LOEB & TIM SALE**

Tim Sale's legendary series, *Hulk Gray* examines the times of The Incredible Hulk™, before the world knew of his connection to scientist Bruce Banner. It revealed hidden mysteries and brought to light some true secrets of the creature. This detailed wall statue depicts the Gray Hulk busting right through a wall and into your home with a myriad of detailed beams, wires, and pipes to complete the effect.

Sculpted by Derek Miller

- Limited to 1,000 pieces

Includes hand-numbered base with matching box and Certificate of Authenticity

MARVEL
www.marvel.com

DIAMOND SELECT TOYS
www.diamondselecttoys.com

COMIC SHOP LOCATOR SERVICE
888-COMIC-BOOK
comicshoplocator.com